Marley & Maverick
The Perfect Tree House

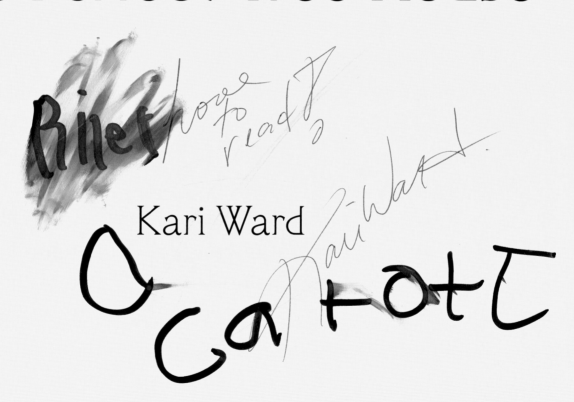

Riley I hope to read

Kari Ward

Carrott

AuthorHouse™

1663 Liberty Drive

Bloomington, IN 47403

www.authorhouse.com

Phone: 1-800-839-8640

First published by AuthorHouse 9/1/2011

ISBN: 978-1-4567-4282-9 (SC)

Library of Congress Control Number: 2011903599

Printed in Canada by Friesens Corporation

Altona, MB

August 2011

67631

This book is printed on acid-free paper.

authorHOUSE®

By: Riley

L Uuuuu

Using their imaginations always came easily for Marley and Maverick.

"Do you want to see my tree house?" asked Maverick.

"I sure do!" replied Marley.

"Close your eyes and come with me," said Maverick, and off they went.

The two adventurers came to a set of beautiful stairs that went round and round a tree.
They climbed as high as the clouds.
"Look, Marley, it's a pink door!" exclaimed Maverick.

They slowly opened the door.

CREAK ...

Inside, it was full of balloons-so many balloons they could not see where they were going!

POP!

A balloon popped on Marley's barrette.
"Let's pop them all!" hollered Maverick.

POP-POP-pop-pop-pop-POP

Just as they popped the last balloon, they realized they were in a fish tank.

In this fish tank, the fish were on the outside, looking in and laughing.
One of the fish was pointing to an elevator.
"Let's go!" exclaimed Marley.

The adventurers ran into the elevator.

ZOOM!

The elevator went so fast, Marley and Maverick could barely hang on.

EEERRRRCH!

When they finally stopped, the door slowly slid open.
Marley and Maverick could not believe their eyes!
It was a magnificent roller coaster!

The roller coaster gave them a ride through the zoo.

All the animals waved and danced. "This is the best day ever!" Marley said in an excited voice.

The roller coaster stopped on top of the tree house. Next to the tree house was a bright, yellow waterslide.

"YAHOO!" the friends hollered with anticipation.

Down they went
through curves and dips
and whoopty whooos!
They were soaked!

SPLASH!

Marley and Maverick hit the water at the bottom and slid all the way home.

"That was great!" exclaimed Marley. "Let's do it again!"

Marley and Maverick closed their eyes and imagined running up the stairs again.

HAVE FUN WITH YOUR IMAGINATION TODAY!
Love,
      Marley & Maverick

KARI WARD is a single mom of two girls. She writes books that make your children want to turn every page. She writes about a young girl and her puppy, who go on amazing adventures. The books will help your children tap into their own imaginations and want more.